The Oak And His Friends

Anna Tyumentseva

One day the little hedgehog was hurrying home with a huge pile of food foraged from the forest. Suddenly it started raining really heavily. In his hurry to get home, the little hedgehog dropped an acorn.

Right where it fell, the acorn hid under a leaf that had dropped
off a tree. Tucked up under this blanket he fell
into a sweet sleep.

He slept for such a long time.
He woke up in the spring when the snow was melting.
He wasn't an acorn any more, he was a little sprig.

The mouse liked the little sprig
and dug a little hole beneath him.

Time passed and the little sprig
turned into a young tree. The bees made a hive
for themselves on the very top branch. The rabbit
and the badger dug sets among his roots.
Then the magpie flew down and made her nest.

Next to arrive was the woodpecker
who pecked out a hole to live in.

Then a spider came along and marked out its place on the oak
with a spider web. They all lived together happily.

The oak liked being a home for them all.
He spent all day from morning to night watching
what his friends were doing.

He slept at night,
but sometimes heard what
his nocturnal residents were
getting up to.

One night, the owl hooted loudly in his crown — Twit Twoo! The oak woke with a start and realised that it had moved into the old hole left by the woodpecker who had moved into a smaller and more cosy one. The oak wasn't cross about being woken up. He saw a family of fireflies flitting around him: such beauty!

As the oak grew so did the number of his friends living there. New nests and dens appeared. Even a bear came and dug a den in a hole next to the oak.

In the autumn the oak's acorns ripened.
The animals and birds were really fond of them
and stored them away for the winter.
They used the fallen leaves to keep
their homes warm.

When the cold days arrived, the oak fell asleep for the whole of the winter. The bear, badger, hedgehog and grass snake slept with him. It's so sweet to sleep beneath the snow!

The rest of the oak's friends carried on with the daily work.

But when it was very very cold, they sat at home to keep warm.

And munched on their stores of tasty acorns.

In the winter the rabbits and partridges changed their coats from grey to white and won all the games of hide and seek with the fox.

As the warm days of spring arrived, everyone woke up.
Everybody got really busy, they had so many things
to do after the long winter.

They needed to wash,

find fresh food,

tidy their houses.

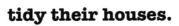

And in the spring the oak blossomed!
It's true that the flowers are very modest. But the bees loved
their nectar and made the most delicious honey from them.

Ask the bear —
he'll tell you!

One hot summer's day, there was a terrible storm. A bolt of lightning struck the oak and its dry bark caught fire! There was a huge commotion. All the oak's friends began to flee.

But they quickly came back, because
the oak was their home! They all worked together
and put out the fire.

To begin with the oak suffered great pain, but the burnt spot
healed very quickly with new bark and branches. A little gap
in the bark was formed and a bat made her home there.
Black was her favourite colour!

One autumn, much later, the oak produced a huge harvest
of acorns and everyone ate to their hearts' content
and filled their stocks for the winter.

The friends decided to say thank you to the oak. They adorned him with flowers, laid out a treat of tasty food at his roots and invited everyone to the celebration.

At dusk just before
the daytime friends had gone
to bed and the night-time
friends had just woken up,
they all danced around the oak
singing happy songs.

The oak thought to himself:
"How old am I?"
He began counting until
he reached — one hundred!
"Happy Birthday,
beloved oak!"

Tyumentseva Anna

The Oak And His Friends

Tyumentseva Anna
tumanna@gmail.com
+91 9765616086

First Edition, May 2020